The
Declaration of Independence

A Level Three Reader

By Cynthia Klingel and Robert B. Noyed

The
Child's
World

On the cover...
This is a photo of the Declaration of Independence.

Published by The Child's World®, Inc.
PO Box 326
Chanhassen, MN 55317-0326
800-599-READ
www.childsworld.com

Photo Credits
© CORBIS: 5, 9, 10, 29
© Hulton Archives: 13
© North Wind Pictures: 6, 21, 22, 25
© Photri, Inc.: 26
© Stock Montage: 14, 17
© Tony Freeman/PhotoEdit: cover, 18

Project Coordination: Editorial Directions, Inc.
Photo Research: Alice K. Flanagan

Library of Congress Cataloging-in-Publication Data
Klingel, Cynthia Fitterer.
The Declaration of Independence / by Cynthia Klingel and Robert B. Noyed.
    p. cm.
ISBN 1-56766-959-X (library bound : alk. paper)
1. United States. Declaration of Independence—Juvenile literature.
2. United States—Politics and government—1775-1783—Juvenile literature.
[1. United States. Declaration of Independence. 2. United States—Politics and government—1775-1783.]
I. Noyed, Robert B. II.Title.
E221 .K58 2001
973.3'13—dc21
                            00-013175

Do you know where the signing of the Declaration of **Independence** took place? Here is a map to help you find out.

3

The Declaration of Independence is an important piece of writing in American history. It was written in 1776. It is the basis for America's government and laws.

This is Thomas Jefferson's early draft of the Declaration of Independence. →

A Declaration by the Representatives of the UNITED STATES OF AMERICA, in General Congress assembled.

When in the course of human events it becomes necessary for one people to dissolve the political bands which have connected them with another, and to assume among the powers of the earth the separate and equal station to which the laws of nature & of nature's god entitle them, a decent respect to the opinions of mankind requires that they should declare the causes which impel them to the separation.

We hold these truths to be self-evident, that all men are created equal, that they are endowed by their creator with equal & inherent & inalienable rights, that among these are life, & liberty, & the pursuit of happiness; that to secure these rights, governments are instituted among men, deriving their just powers from the consent of the governed; that whenever any form of government becomes destructive of these ends, it is the right of the people to alter or to abolish it, & to institute new government, laying it's foundation on such principles & organising it's powers in such form, as to them shall seem most likely to effect their safety & happiness. prudence indeed will dictate that governments long established should not be changed for light & transient causes: and accordingly all experience hath shewn that mankind are more disposed to suffer while evils are sufferable, than to right themselves by abolishing the forms to which they are accustomed. but when a long train of abuses & usurpations [begun at a distinguished period, &] pursuing invariably the same object, evinces a design to reduce them under absolute Despotism, it is their right, it is their duty, to throw off such + & to provide new guards for their future security. such has

5

6

In 1776, the **colonists** in America were fighting with England. This fighting was called the Revolutionary War. The colonists were trying to win their freedom from England. They did not want others to make their laws. They wanted to make their own laws.

This is a drawing of colonists removing signs of British rule.

In 1774, the colonists had decided that England would never give them freedom. Twelve of the thirteen **colonies** chose people to meet together to decide what to do. The colony of Georgia did not send anyone.

Here you can see a map of the thirteen colonies. →

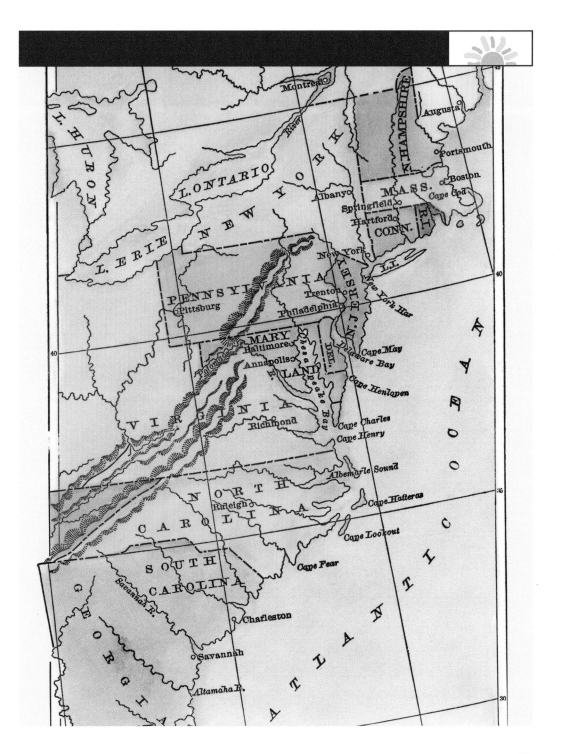

9

This group of colonists was called the Continental Congress. The colonists wanted very much to win their freedom and govern themselves. The Continental Congress met again in 1775 to discuss the colonies' problems with England.

This is the building where the Continental Congress met.

Finally, the Continental Congress voted to **declare** the colonies' independence from England. The members decided to do this in writing. A small group would need to write this very important paper.

This picture shows a printed record of the first Continental Congress. →

JOURNAL

OF THE

PROCEEDINGS

OF THE

CONGRESS,

Held at PHILADELPHIA,

September 5, 1774.

Five men were chosen. They were John Adams, Benjamin Franklin, Thomas Jefferson, Robert Livingston, and Roger Sherman. One man had to write the first **draft**. Young Thomas Jefferson was chosen because he was smart and good at writing.

Here you can see the five authors of the Declaration of Independence.

Thomas Jefferson spent two weeks writing the declaration. He worked hard to explain why the colonies wanted their freedom. He tried to explain the rights the colonists believed they should have.

This is a drawing of Thomas Jefferson. →

17

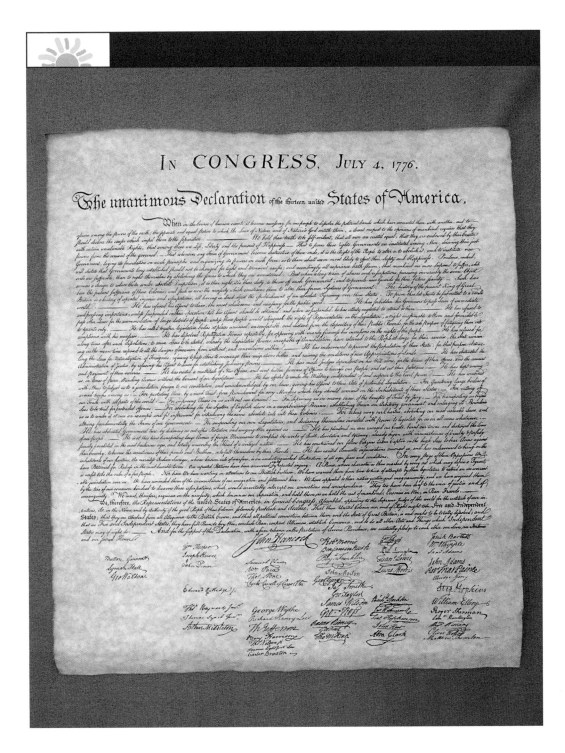

The Declaration of Independence describes how one type of government should work. This type of government is called a **democracy**. The United States has been a democracy since 1776.

In the Declaration of Independence, Jefferson also wrote about the rights that people should have. Jefferson said that people are born with these rights and that no one should take them away.

This is a drawing of Americans →
meeting to discuss their rights.

21

These rights included the right to live, to be free, and to seek happiness. Jefferson's draft of the Declaration of Independence also talked about the job of the government.

This drawing shows the reading of the Declaration of Independence to the public.

Thomas Jefferson thought it was important to explain why the colonies wanted their freedom from England. He wrote about how the king had taken away the rights of the colonists.

Here you can see colonists tearing down a statue of the king of England.

Thomas Jefferson did an excellent job. The members of the Continental Congress liked what he had written. On July 4, 1776, the members signed the Declaration of Independence. America now considered itself free from England.

This painting shows the signing of the Declaration of Independence.

The Declaration of Independence changed the lives of people in America. Today, more than 200 years later, it is still important to democracy in the United States. You can see the original Declaration of Independence at the National Archives Building in Washington, D.C.

These people are reading the original Declaration of Independence in Washington, D.C.

Glossary

colonies (KOL-uh-neez)
Colonies are lands ruled by a
faraway country.

colonists (KOL-uh-nists)
Colonists are people who live
in a colony.

declare (dih-KLAYR)
When you declare something, you
say it firmly.

democracy (deh-MOK-ruh-see)
In a democracy, people vote for
their leaders.

draft (DRAFT)
A draft is a first rough copy of
something written.

independence (in-deh-PEN-denss)
Independence means freedom.

Index

To Find Out More

Books

Dalgliesh, Alice. *The Fourth of July Story.* New York: Aladdin, 1995.

Fradin, Dennis Brindell. *The Thirteen Colonies.* Danbury, Conn.: Children's Press, 1988.

Giblin, James Cross. *Fireworks, Picnics and Flags.* New York: Houghton Mifflin, 1983.

Web Sites

The Declaration of Independence of the United States of America
http://www.nara.gov/exhall/charters/declaration/decmain.html
For information about visiting the National Archives Building to see the declaration.

Independence National Historical Park
http://www.nps.gov/inde/exindex.htm
To find out more about where the Declaration of Independence was signed.

The White House Site on the Declaration of Independence
http://www.house.gov/house/Declaration.html
To read the full text of the Declaration of Independence.

Note to Parents and Educators

Welcome to The Wonders of Reading™! These books provide text at three different levels for beginning readers to practice and strengthen their reading skills. In addition, the use of nonfiction text gives readers the valuable opportunity to *read to learn*, not just to learn to read.

These leveled readers allow children to choose books at their level of reading confidence and performance. Level One books offer beginning readers simple language, word choice, and sentence structure as well as a word list. Level Two books feature slightly more difficult vocabulary, longer sentences, and longer total text. In the back of each Level Two book are an index and a list of books and Web sites for finding out more information. Level Three books continue to extend word choice and length of text. In the back of each Level Three book are a glossary, an index, and a list of books and Web sites for further research.

State and national standards in reading and language arts emphasize using nonfiction at all levels of reading development. The Wonders of Reading™ books fill the historical void in nonfiction for primary grade readers with the additional benefit of a leveled text.

About the Authors

Cynthia Klingel has worked as a high school English teacher and an elementary teacher. She is currently the curriculum director for a Minnesota school district. Writing children's books is another way for her to continue her passion for sharing the written word with children. Cynthia is a frequent visitor to the children's section of bookstores and enjoys spending time with her many friends, family, and two daughters.

Robert Noyed started his career as a newspaper reporter. Since then, he has worked in communications and public relations for more than fourteen years for a Minnesota school district. He enjoys writing books for children and finds that it brings a different feeling of challenge and accomplishment from other writing projects. He is an avid reader who also enjoys music, theater, traveling, and spending time with his wife, son, and daughter.